PE  M

Based on *The Railway Series* by the Rev. W. Awdry

Illustrations by
Robin Davies and Jerry Smith

EGMONT

EGMONT

We bring stories to life

First published in Great Britain 2005
by Egmont Books Limited
239 Kensington High Street, London W8 6SA
All Rights Reserved

Thomas the Tank Engine & Friends

A BRITT ALLCROFT COMPANY PRODUCTION

Based on The Railway Series by The Rev W Awdry

ISBN 1 4052 1715 4
5 7 9 10 8 6 4
Printed in Great Britain

This is a story about Peter Sam, a Narrow-Gauge Engine. He first worked at the Old Railway for The Thin Controller many years ago. Everyone made fun of his new funnel, but he soon had the last laugh …

It was winter on the Island of Sodor. Peter Sam was puffing slowly along the track.

He was worried about his funnel. It had not felt right since he had had an accident with some trucks, and now it felt like the wind was trying to blow it off.

"My funnel feels all wobbly," he said to his Driver. "I wish my new one would hurry up and arrive. The Thin Controller said it will be something special!"

"You and your special funnel," laughed Rusty, Sir Handel and Duncan. They all liked Peter Sam but his special funnel had become a bit of a joke.

The winter wind grew stronger and rain lashed down on the engines. The heavy rain turned the hillside streams into raging rivers which threatened to wash away the tracks.

Rusty worked hard carrying workmen up and down the line to clear the branches and leaves so the water could flow away from the tracks.

The next day, Rusty's Driver brought bad news. "There's been a washout near the tunnel," he said. "The track bed has been swept away. We need to repair it immediately!"

The repair work took much longer than expected. As the days went by, the weather became much colder and frosty. Finally, the repairs were finished so the tunnel could be used again.

The next morning, Peter Sam carefully went over the mended track and slowly rolled into the dark tunnel.

His Driver shouted, "There's something hanging from the roof!"

There was a loud clanging noise and Peter Sam suddenly felt rather strange. As he came out of the tunnel, his Driver saw that he had lost his funnel!

Peter Sam's Guard went back into the tunnel to find his funnel. He came out holding the funnel and a large icicle.

"This is what hit you!" he said. "We can't mend your funnel here, we'll have to finish the journey without it and get it repaired at the station."

Peter Sam set off again but, without his funnel, smoke billowed over the carriages and the passengers complained.

At the side of the track, his Driver noticed an old drainpipe. He wired it to Peter Sam to work as a funnel for the rest of the journey. Peter Sam was embarrassed.

"I hope none of the other engines see me looking like this," he said sadly.

But as Peter approached the station, Rusty and Sir Handel saw his drainpipe funnel. They burst into laughter and sang a song:

Peter Sam's said again and again,
His new funnel will put ours to shame.
But he went into a tunnel,
And lost his old funnel,
Now his famous special funnel's a drain!

Luckily for Peter Sam, his new funnel had arrived that day. He couldn't wait to see it, but when his Driver opened the parcel he thought there had been a mistake.

"Oh, no! Has somebody squashed my new funnel?" asked Peter Sam.

The Thin Controller laughed. "Don't worry," he said. "It's a special funnel, called a Giesl. It is the most up-to-date funnel there is!"

"How does it work?" asked Peter Sam.

"When you puff, you draw air through your fire to make it burn brightly. Your old funnel made puffing hard work, but your new Giesl funnel has special pipes to help the air come easily. You'll now have more strength to do your work."

Peter Sam wasn't sure that he was going to like having the strange new funnel.

At first, the other engines thought Peter Sam's new funnel was a great joke.

"Did you sit on it?" asked Duncan and hooted with laughter.

"It's certainly *special*!" giggled Sir Handel.

Peter Sam had wished he had his old funnel back but he soon realized that The Thin Controller had been right. His new funnel did make work much easier. Now the other engines would have nothing to laugh about.

Peter Sam became very proud of his new funnel. It helped him glide along the tracks, easily pulling long lines of trucks behind him.

Sir Handel, Duncan and Rusty soon stopped laughing at his new funnel. They watched in amazement as he sped past them, pulling more trucks than he had ever been able to before. The other engines wished they also had a special funnel just like Peter Sam!

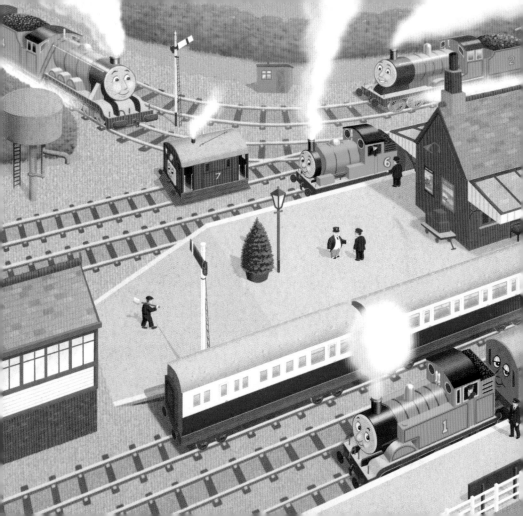

The Thomas Story Library is THE definitive collection of stories about Thomas and ALL his Friends.

5 more Thomas Story Library titles will be chuffing into your local bookshop in April 2006:

´Arry and Bert
George
Jack
Annie and Clarabel
Rheneas

And there are even more
Thomas Story Library books to follow later!
So go on, start your Thomas Story Library NOW!

A Fantastic Offer for Thomas the Tank Engine Fans!

STICK
POUND
COIN
HERE

In every Thomas Story Library book like this one, you will find a special token. Collect 6 Thomas tokens and we will send you a brilliant Thomas poster, and a double-sided bedroom door hanger!

Simply tape a £1 coin in the space above, and fill out the form overleaf.

Cut along the dotted line

TO BE COMPLETED BY AN ADULT

To apply for this great offer, ask an adult to complete the coupon below
and send it with a pound coin and 6 tokens, to:
THOMAS OFFERS, PO BOX 715, HORSHAM RH12 5WG

☐ Please send a Thomas poster and door hanger. I enclose 6 tokens
plus a £1 coin. (Price includes P&P)

Fan's name...

Address..

....Postcode............................

Date of birth...

Name of parent/guardian..

Signature of parent/guardian...

Please allow 28 days for delivery. Offer is only available while stocks last. We reserve the right to change
the terms of this offer at any time and we offer a 14 day money back guarantee. This does not affect your
statutory rights.

☐ Data Protection Act: If you do not wish to receive other similar offers from us or companies we
recommend, please tick this box. Offers apply to UK only.

Cut along the dotted line